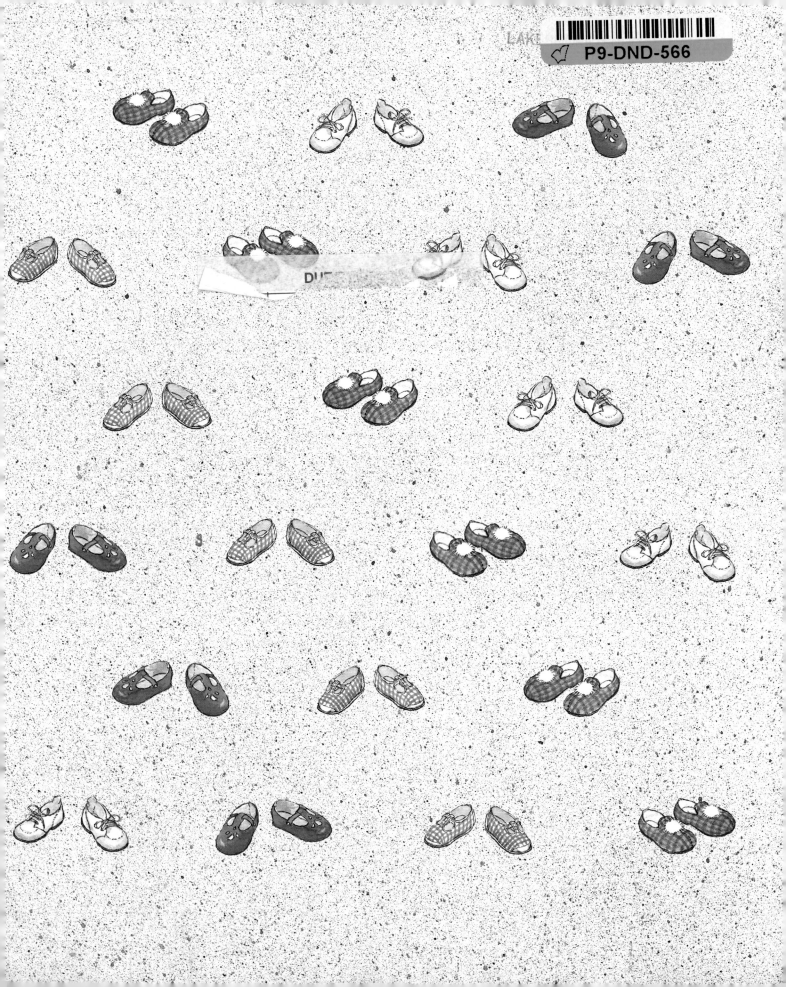

*For Mara and Marissa*
**M.W.**


*For Sarah, Rowan, Rachel,*
*Helen, Sarah W. and Charlie…*
*Giants to be.*
**P.D.**

Published by Delacorte Press
Bantam Doubleday Dell Publishing Group, Inc.
666 Fifth Avenue, New York, New York 10103

This work was originally published in Great Britain by Walker Books Ltd., London

Library of Congress Cataloging-in-Publication-Data
Waddell, Martin.
Once there were giants.
Summary: As a baby girl grows up and becomes an adult,
the "giants" in her family seem to grow smaller.
[1. Growth—Fiction.   2. Family life—Fiction]
I. Dale, Penny, ill.   II. Title.
PZ7. W1137On        1989        [E]        88–33586
ISBN 0-385-29806-4

Manufactured in Italy
First U.S.A. printing October 1989
10   9   8   7   6   5   4   3   2   1

# Once There Were
# GIANTS

Written by Martin Waddell

Illustrated by Penny Dale

**Delacorte Press**

Once there were Giants in our house.
There were Mom and Dad and
Jill and John and Uncle Tom.

The small one on the rug is me.

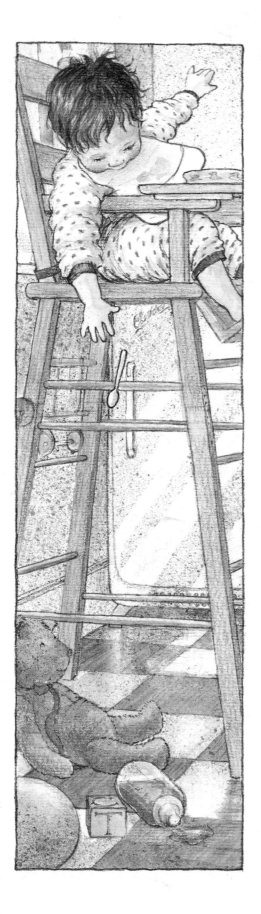

When I could sit up
Mom bought a high chair.
I sat at the table
way up in the sky
with Mom and Dad and
Jill and John and Uncle Tom.

The one throwing oatmeal is me.

When I could crawl
I crawled on the floor.
Dad was a dragon and
he gave a roar that scared
Jill and John and Uncle Tom.

The one who is crying is me.

When I could walk

I walked to the park with

Jill and John and Uncle Tom.

We fed the ducks and

Jill stood on her head.

The one in the duck pond is me.

When I could talk
I talked and talked!
I annoyed Uncle Tom and
got sat on by Jill and by John.
That's John on my head
and Jill on my knee.

The one stretching out is me!

When I could run
I ran and ran,
chased by Mom and Dad
and Uncle Tom and
Jill on her bike and
my brother John.

The one who is puffing is me.

When I went to nursery school
I wouldn't play games and
I called people names and
upset water on Millie Magee.
She's the one with the towel.

The one being scolded is me!

When I went to school
I was bigger by then.
Mom had to leave at
a quarter to ten and
she didn't come back
for a long, long time.
I didn't shout and
I didn't scream.
She came for me at
a quarter to three.

The one on Mom's knee is me.

When I went to sixth grade
I had lots of fun.
I got big and strong
and punched my brother John.
He's the one with the sore nose.

The one with the black eye is me.

When I went to high school
I was taller than Mom,
and nearly as tall as my uncle Tom.
But I never caught up
with my brother John.
I ran and I jumped
and they all came to see.
There they are cheering.

The one who's winning is me.

When I went to work
I lived all by myself.
Then I met Don and we married.
There's Jill and John
and Uncle Tom
and Mom's the one crying,
and Dad is the one
with the beer on his head.

The bride looking happy is me!

Then we had a baby girl
and things changed.
There are Giants in our house again!
There is my husband, Don,
and Jill and John,
my mom and my dad
and Uncle Tom
and one of the Giants is...

ME!

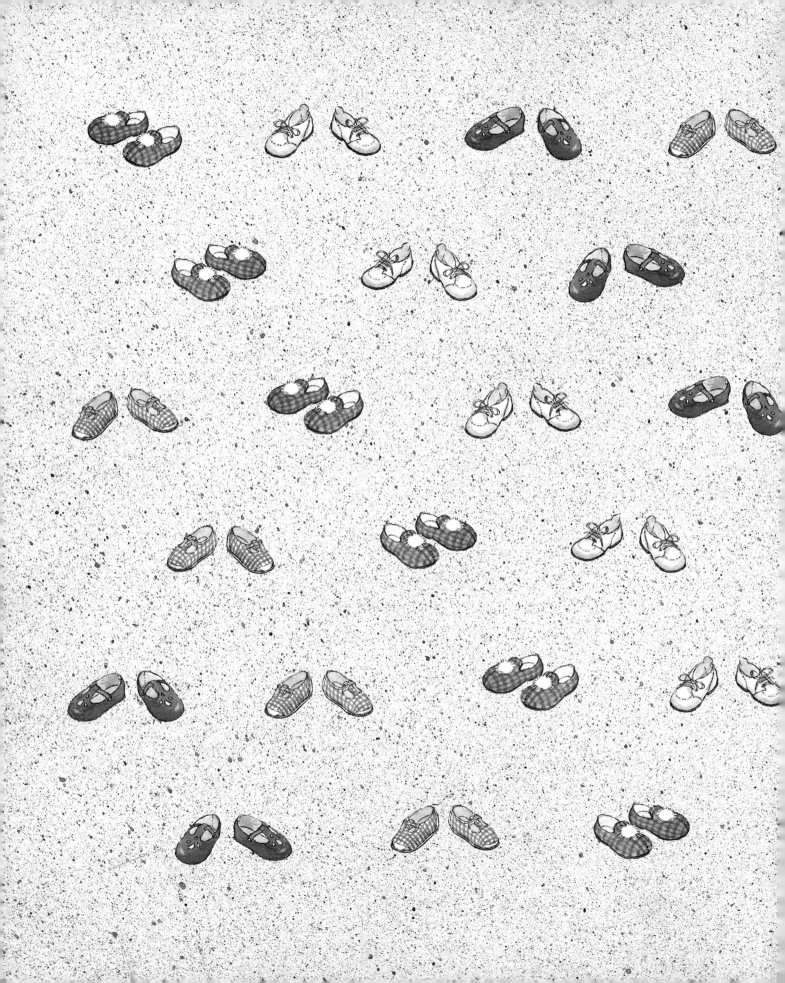